MW00614834

Tiny Twisted Tales

By Darby Lee Patterson

COPYRIGHT

ISBN: 9780692096222

Bolton Road Publishing
P.O. Box 556
Pollock Pines, CA 95726

Bolton Road
PUBLISHING

For Randall with his constant support and Geri Esposito for encouragement when needed, and for the psychotherapist who read one of my stories and seriously asked me, "For how long have you wanted to kill people?"

Table of Contents

Introduction

I've always loved mysteries, particularly those with memorable characters and a plot that doesn't depend on long bloody passages regarding the victim's manner and condition in death. My mystery novel, "The Song of Jackass Creek," is written in a style reminiscent of classic works based on rich storytelling, rather than graphic violence. I am very pleased with the many Five Star reviews I'm getting from people who also appreciate this approach.

You're about to read something a little different! The short stories in "Tiny Twisted Tales" also focus on character but reflect the wicked sense of humor I enjoyed in works by Hitchcock and Rod Serling, among others. There's a dark humor in my 'twisted' stories but I think you'll also find sympathy for the women who find a way of 'getting by with getting even.' After all, haven't we all wanted to do that from time to time?

Darby Lee Patterson

The Goody-Goody Girl

Charlene finished packing bags of food for the homeless and disadvantaged by two on a Saturday afternoon. It was one of many volunteer activities she did throughout the week. Wednesday nights she visited a convalescent home to read to the residents, Sunday mornings she taught religion classes at the Neuman Center after Mass and she also did bookkeeping for a group that worked with troubled teens.

With few exceptions, Charlene had spent forty-some years of her life dedicated to being very, very good. This required lots of giving and sacrifice, no cursing or drinking, shunning impure thoughts, and the telling of no lies.

Charlene also stayed away from the sins of immodesty and vanity. Her skirts reached mid-calf, necklines always hugged her collarbone. Her only make-up was a touch of pink blush and lipstick.

She was neither attractive nor unattractive. Her light chestnut hair had dulled over the years and she wore it pulled back in a loose braid, much like her mother before her. Charlene had lovely green eyes with brown flecks that, in a certain light, looked like gold dust. With near perfect teeth, had she smiled more often, she would have been perceived as pretty instead of plain.

Spiritual value fueled Charlene and she once believed that her life of good works and self-sacrifice would be rewarded. Still, when not busy with her volunteer work or her job as a data processor, Charlene spent her time waiting. Waiting for romance, for happiness, for life to happen to her. Consequently, she didn't smile much and seldom laughed out loud. Premature frown lines had begun to form at the corners of her mouth and she sensed her whole face slowly falling.

Occasionally, as she'd gotten older, she felt a sense of disquiet building in the hollow of her chest when she saw other women. Women who swore, smoked, plastered on the makeup, and were loose with men. Women with no morals. Yet, they were laughing while she sat in her neat little house alone reading mystery novels for excitement.

Slowly, over the course of months, new, disturbing feelings started to emerge. Feelings directed to those very people to whom she'd devoted volunteer efforts so faithfully for so many years. Saturdays, she found herself looking at the people in the food lines with disdain. She wondered how they could be so weak in character and so willing to take, take, take. Surely, some of them could find jobs and provide for themselves?

She felt repulsion creeping under her skin at the old

folk's home as the smells of age and infirmity gnawed at her senses. Where were their families? Why was it up to her to hold frail and wrinkled hands as addled minds spun nonsensical stories? Why did some of them even keep on living?

Her patience grew shortest with the troubled teens. Their self-centeredness, rudeness and utter lack of gratitude incited anger inside her. She, Charlene, had never behaved like that for one day in her life! If she had, her mother would have made sure it never, ever happened again.

In addition to the intrusion of these unwelcome thoughts, a shadow of doubt descended over the core of Charlene's being – her faith. Increasingly, she doubted the truth of the lessons she taught to recent converts at the church. She heard herself mouth the words and then, simultaneously, ask herself the doubting question. She began to feel like a hypocrite.

And then came the month when everything started to change. The flow of good and truth came forth like water from a blessed fountain. The dark thoughts evaporated in the purity of sunlight as a page turned and someone entered her life to forever alter its course. His name was Dwight and he appeared one Sunday in her class, a Catholic convert wanting to learn more about the faith. That first encounter had been more like a thrill ride at an amusement park than a simple conversation about the beatitudes. Dwight had remained after class, one which Charlene thought she'd taught rather badly.

"Well then," he'd said from the school desk where he was sitting, "if God is all knowing and all good, then how can He let evil exist in the world?" He leaned back, folded his arms across his chest and smiled challengingly at Charlene.

She gave him an abbreviated answer about free will and man's ability "indeed, responsibility" to choose between good and evil. Throughout the exchange, she had moved closer to him and noticed that he had no sight in his left eye which was scarred and clouded over with a milky film. It made her soften her demeanor toward him.

When he introduced himself, Charlene extended her hand and he took it with his left in an awkward handshake. "Sorry," he explained. "Another little present I got in Nam. Not much on the right side of this body is much good." She noticed then that his smile was charmingly crooked, much wider on the left than the right. Charlene sat down and the carnival ride began.

That afternoon, they went for coffee at the donut shop near the Cathedral. He invited her to see a movie on the following Tuesday, dinner on Thursday and on Saturday he helped her fill bags of groceries for the poor. Within that first week, she memorized his face. Every line and crease, the outline of shadow where his beard started to grow at the end of the day. On Sunday before Mass, she lit a candle for him and said a prayer of thanks and of contrition for her former doubts.

The days flew by like monarchs dancing gracefully on the wind and Charlene let love happen. She had no idea of what Dwight actually looked like to the rest of the world - only that he was beautiful to her. She listened to his stories of the war with compassion and understanding. He was a decorated hero, worked at the local VA hospital and had been born in Florida where some of his family still lived.

She let him become intimate with her, in fact wanted the closeness and was embarrassed by her ravenous desire. It hadn't felt wrong and she wondered why she'd lived all those years condemning the passion she now craved.

Dwight, she realized, was the man she'd waited for, worked for, her entire life. And he for her. With his physical and emotional scars he needed a woman of great capacity to nurture and care for him. There was no one more giving than Charlene and finally she had found someone to shower with her abundant compassion. Her reward was late in coming, but Dwight was worth the wait. He completed her.

Within two short weeks, they'd connected like lost pieces of a puzzle. "Funny," he mused while holding her hand, "I can't see out of one eye, can't use an arm and have a bum leg but, for the first time in my life, I feel complete." Charlene cried tears of ultimate joy and dedicated herself to his happiness.

Dwight talked about a day in the near future when they might become engaged. He said he was saving for a ring but had to get past a few financial challenges first. Charlene didn't want to pry, so she asked no questions about what those challenges might be.

They were marking their first month anniversary when Dwight told Charlene he would have to go away for a short time. The financial challenges he'd spoken about had become urgent, he said, and he needed to raise the kind of money that wasn't available to him locally. Charlene felt as if someone had kicked her in the stomach. The thought of Dwight leaving was unbearable. She saw the turrets of her candy castle toppling.

Before she even knew the nature of his crisis, she offered him a loan. There was ample equity in her house to cover his needs and Charlene quickly made plans to get a loan of one-hundred-thousand dollars. Dwight seemed amazed at her generosity, speechless. She felt calm and gratified.

"I guess there was a reason God left me that house," she said lightly. "He knew that we would need it someday."

Dwight vowed to pay it all back. He needed it for his brother, he explained. Heart surgery that would save his life. They would be married when this was all over with.

Charlene pictured the two of them, tucked away in her house, working together. They'd paint the walls a bright color, one her mother would have hated. They'd plant a garden; he'd fix the little things she'd ignored while living alone.

She called the bank. With her perfect credit history and home equity, she had the loan in only two weeks. Two weeks that had been like a fairy tale. Dwight treated her like a princess - cooking dinners, pampering her, fixing the squeaky hinge on the screen door of her house. It was with pride and deep satisfaction that she handed him the cashier's check for one-hundred thousand dollars.

Charlene knew the five days in which Dwight would be gone to Florida to help his brother would be tough for her. She thought about the adage "absence makes the heart grow fonder," and didn't believe it possible. She busied herself with housework and plans for their future.

Of course, Charlene fully expected Dwight to phone her a few times. He didn't. Nor did he return after five days. More than a week after his departure, Charlene set out to contact him, give him a chance to explain. Failing to reach him, Charlene made a few other calls and discovered information that somewhere in the recesses of her mind, she already knew. There had been no Dwight W. Lucas enlisted in the U.S. Army. He had not served in Vietnam or anywhere else in the Armed Forces. His brother had never been in the Tampa Cardiac Center and Dwight never worked at the local VA hospital.

Charlene knew that she should call the police. However, the specter of being a middle-aged spinster fool in public was unacceptable, unbearable. Instead, she called in sick at work and stayed home for seven straight days. There, she sat in a chair facing her living room window and simply stared outside. At night, she didn't bother to turn on the lights and was satisfied to sit in the darkness until she moved into her bedroom to struggle with her dreams. She ate little and slept fitfully. Her mind buzzed

7

with questions and tortured thoughts.

She looked back on her lifetime of good works, of resisting temptation and remaining true to the principles her mother taught her with such relentless, often painful, discipline. Charlene - the clean, pure, generous, sacrificing, selfless, helpful soul.

She let the anger build until it could be contained no longer and burst forth as rage within the beige walls of her house. "What has being good gotten me!" she demanded, shaking her fists at heaven. "I'm unhappy. I'm a fool! This is what the goody-goody girl gets!"

By the end of the week, she had shouted and cried herself out and uttered every cruel thought that marched across her mind. When it was over, Charlene emerged drained of unhappiness. Inside her, there was an empty place where a reservoir of tears once waited to spill over in a torrent. She filled that void with new emotions, with growing determination to radically change her destiny. To put the goody-goody girl out of her misery like a mortally wounded bird.

By the following Monday, her plan was formed and she was ready to play out the charade of her former life. People wouldn't notice at first that she had changed - the physical transition, she decided, would have to be gradual. All those things she'd shunned as unworthy a good woman - the makeup, provocative clothing, a lifestyle of personal freedom and moral flexibility - would eventually be integrated into her new life. She wouldn't let it happen overnight because that might draw unwanted attention.

8

She decided to start with something simple – maybe a new hairdo. (No more braids!) Little by little the mouse would be devoured by the lioness.

But before she went completely public with her physical transformation, Charlene intended to alter the core of her being and commit the ultimate act of evil - an extreme that would counterbalance her past life. There was logic in her thought that, since radical goodness had reaped only loneliness and disappointment, the opposite might be a catalyst to happiness, pleasure, satisfaction. Based on her avid reading of crime and mystery novels, she began plotting the perfect murder.

The plotting wasn't difficult. In fact, she found it rather enjoyable. She carefully considered her own physical strength, what methods best suited her temperament, how to dispose of a body so that it would never be found and other details that could be researched in her own extensive library of paperbacks.

Back at data processing again, she appeared with a new but modest hairdo cut in a feathered style, and lipstick a shade darker than before. No one took notice.

After two weeks of preparation, she was ready to launch a new life. It was a Saturday night when she cautiously applied a layer of makeup to her face. She then brightened her mysterious eyes to emphasize the golden flecks and painted a glossy red on her full lips, lining them with a shade darker pencil. She'd gotten books and practiced for days ahead of time after work, experimenting with different looks and colors until a nearly unrecognizable Charlene stared back at her in the mirror.

She pulled her hair up off her neck and pinned it atop her head in coquettish curls that reminded her of women in the Clark Gable version of "Gone with the Wind." The skirt and blouse she'd bought for the occasion were unlike anything she'd ever owned - youthful, bright, the skirt showing her knees and displaying the womanly curves of her body.

She was nearly stunned at the final product and stood in front of her full-length mirror repeatedly turning and glancing at the reflection over her shoulder as if it might disappear should she lose sight of herself. Finally, unable to contain the pleasure she felt, Charlene smiled provocatively at her reflection and said out loud, "You are what they call a knockout!" This, having a double meaning, made her laugh and feel a sense of power.

She checked her house to make certain everything was ready and went into the basement for one last look at the tools. She propped open the little door that covered the water heater right at the bottom of the cement stairs and obscured the rest of the basement from sight. She pulled the metal chain on the light and cast the basement into darkness; she then reached up and unscrewed the light bulb. The contrast between the living room where fresh flowers, elegant drink glasses, and seductive lighting awaited her guest and the stark basement with its power tools and bare hundred-watt bulb suspended from the ceiling was radical. Upstairs exuded feminine warmth and comfort while just below a cold, damp death chamber lie waiting for Charlene's guest.

For the evening, she'd chosen a busy nightclub with a packed dance floor and long chrome bar with high backed stools covered in burgundy velour. She was confident that none of the people she knew in her everyday life would frequent such a place and, if they did, Charlene doubted anyone would recognize her. She balanced herself on a stool near the end of the bar and ordered a drink minus the alcohol.

Within the first hour, several appealing men offered to buy her drinks and tried to strike up conversations. It wasn't until after nine o'clock, however, that Charlene made her selection. He fit all her criteria. Michael was not particularly attractive and not nearly as smooth as many of the men who had approached her. That was how she had planned it. For her act of evil to have full significance, she wanted a genuine victim. Someone basically good, perhaps even a little pitiful. If she were to eliminate a slime like Dwight, she would be doing the world a favor and that was not Charlene's intention.

She let Michael buy her drinks but only sipped at them, dumping the contents now and then to keep the appearance of partying along with him. When he was clearly affected by his drinks, Charlene suggested they go to her house for a "nightcap." She'd had to practice saying that word ahead of time as if it was a foreign language. Michael seemed stunned by his apparent good luck and easily accepted her offer along with the suggestion that they take her car, leaving his in the parking lot.

Once inside her house, Charlene noticed that Michael seemed more relaxed and in command than he had in the bar. He lounged on the mint green, brocade couch as if it were his own and looked at her with undisguised lust. She began to enjoy herself and smiled with anticipation of the evening they would have. Michael sipped his drink and reached out for her, confident his move would be welcome. Charlene let herself slide down on the couch beside him and fingered the silk handkerchief that decorated the pocket of his jacket. "Since we both know where this night is going to end up," she said in a voice rich in promise, "why don't we make it as pleasurable as possible?"

Michael's eyes glowed with intensity and she felt his body flush warm as she suggested they take a bath together. "I have some bath oils and candles. I'll rub your back and other places you might enjoy," she purred, rolling the handkerchief around her index finger. "But, I need your help with one little thing. The pilot light on the water heater went out and maybe you can light it for us? By the time we have another drink, there'll be plenty of hot water for a long, deep bath." Her red lips parted and framed her perfect teeth in an alluring smile.

Michael pulled the silk from her fingers and stuffed the handkerchief back into his pocket. "Water heaters just happen to be a specialty of mine," he said with a grin, "along with lighting several other things." Charlene noticed that more confidence and sexual innuendo had crept into his voice and she wanted to slap him. She could hardly wait.

They walked into the kitchen where Charlene turned on the light which cast a beam down the basement stairs. She handed Michael a box of wooden matches and held a flashlight in her hand, explaining the bulb in the basement had burned out. Another project, she laughed, for a handyman, emphasizing the "handy" for effect.

Michael removed his sports coat and draped it over the back of a kitchen chair. He let Charlene lead him down the stairs where she spread a sheet of heavy mil plastic on the floor for him. "So you don't get your pants soiled," she said. He dropped to his knees in front of the water heater.

He took the flashlight from Charlene and peered behind the metal cover at the foot of the cylinder. Charlene used the time to reach behind the open door and grab a twenty-five-pound sledgehammer. She held it with both hands behind her back until Michael propped up the flashlight to illuminate the pilot, and opened the box of matches. While his attention was entirely focused on the task of reaching into the small space with a lighted match, Charlene raised the iron mallet over her head and swung.

There was a muffled cracking sound as his left temple shattered and his body collapsed into a ridiculous position that nearly made Charlene laugh. The rounded edges of the hammer hadn't broken much skin and, as she had planned, the initial loss of blood was manageable, caught on the plastic beneath him.

Energized by her success, Charlene easily dragged the body on the plastic to the center of the basement where she was prepared to complete her plan. She added more plastic and arranged it to form a channel leading to the laundry drain in the middle of the cement floor. Heavy-duty garbage bags and ties were laid out next to the rain gear she'd found at the surplus store - a long yellow jacket over matching bib overalls. A piece of half-inch plywood stood propped against the window that faced her back-yard. After the hard part was done, Charlene would use it as a ramp to pull the bags up from the basement and out to the yard for loading into her small truck. The Sawz-All was plugged in and the rest of the night stretched before her.

It was nearly three in the morning when she finished. She'd filled five doubled-up garbage bags with Michael, her work clothes, the plastic and anything else used in the project. She arranged the load at the bottom of the win-dow attaching a rope to the first bag so it would easily slide up her ramp. She closed the door to the basement with a sense of satisfaction, and ample energy to clean up any shred of Michael left in her house. She immediately noticed his jacket draped over the kitchen chair and fetched another plastic bag to hold it. Her only indulgence was to remove the silk handkerchief from the pocket to keep as a memento of her total transformation.

Sunday was again filled with nervous anticipation that fueled her energy. She attended Mass and taught the religion class with renewed enthusiasm, striving to keep her emerging personality from bubbling forth. Occasion-ally she pictured what she'd left behind - the air condi-tioner blasted air from the dining room to the kitchen and into the open basement door, keeping the environment cool. The garbage bags were covered with other clear bags of ice to further ensure the delayed disintegration of the contents. After dark, she would load the pickup and go to the food bank, unlock the dumpster and toss her load inside. At approximately 6 a.m. on Monday morning the garbage trucks would come and haul the entire contents to the landfill. The bags would be mixed with tons of other bags in an untraceable garbage heap of unidentifiable smells.

The entire plan proceeded without a single snag. Charlene enjoyed the physical work and felt more alive than she had in years. Driving home from the food bank, Charlene thought of how clever and thorough she'd been, using leverage to compensate for her lack of physical strength, making several small packages from one large and unwieldy object, using effective tools and, still, remaining the mild-mannered, helpful spinster that everyone knew her to be. She'd done all this and accomplished her goal - she'd done an evil act to a somewhat ordinary man and was going to get away with it. She could feel her fate changing and a world of possibilities opening up to her. Charlene was a woman with a new attitude and, soon, she'd start enjoying the rewards.

Over the next two weeks, she occasionally thought it strange that there had been no news about a missing person, although she generally avoided newspapers and TV reports, finding them too filled with violence and negativity. Finally, she assumed her victim had been an out-of-towner and put him out of her mind. Then the came the sharp knock on her door.

"Hello Miss, it's Deputy Clipper from the Sheriff's Department. Could we have a word with you, please?"

Charlene briefly froze in her tracks and then slipped the chain from the door. She was absolutely confident about the integrity of her work and decided there was nothing to fear. She faced two deputies who smiled apologetically.

"Sorry for bothering you ma'am," said the officer whose ID badge identified him as Ted Clipper. "But we're talking to every woman in the neighborhood as a precaution."

"What about?" Charlene politely asked. "This is a very quiet area and we never have any trouble."

"Well, that's been the history," Clipper said, "but I'm afraid we've had some incidents you need to be aware of. Give her one of those flyers, Dave."

The other deputy, with Dave Mendoza printed on his ID badge, peeled a piece of paper from the top of a small stack and handed it to Charlene. "This is an Identikit composite of a man who has been raping and murdering women in the city," Mendoza said. "Last month, he hit a victim only four blocks away from here. We found her car in a parking lot downtown. It was pretty brutal."

Clipper again took over. "Honestly ma'am, this guy is a sicko. I won't go into details but let me tell you we have trouble putting the pieces of his victims together. We need to advise you to have extra caution; lock your doors and call us right away if you hear or see anyone suspicious."

Charlene looked at the black and white image, and held her breath.

"This one's real dangerous ma'am," Deputy Mendoza was saying. "Seems to really enjoy himself. Just to let you know how serious he is, the guy writes a few of words in the victim's blood and then ties the note on the body with a fancy silk hanky ... I'm not at liberty to say what he writes."

"I'll tell you, when we get this guy, there's a bunch of us who would like to see him drawn and quartered," Clipper said, shaking his head. "You be careful now, hear?"

Once the officers left, Charlene leaned against the closed door and let reality seep through her body. It could have been her. Michael - or whatever his name was - had picked her. And, she had picked him. She had executed a killer. Done the world a favor.

The longer she thought about it, the worse she began to feel. She went to the dresser drawer where she had the souvenir silk hankie tucked away. She ran it through her fingers and brought it to her lips. Then, watching herself in the dresser mirror, she bit the end of the red silk and began to tear at it. Furiously, as tears fell, she shredded the trademark memento and went into the bathroom where she watched the filmy pieces of silk circle the toilet bowl and flush into oblivion.

Along the Garden Path

She sat alone at the table in the dimly lit cafe. As usual, she had a book opened and a pen and a tablet of lined paper in front of her. Slowly, the other tables were beginning to fill up with mostly couples who had come, like Gina, to listen to the mellow and expert guitarist that played every Thursday night.

She didn't mind sitting alone anymore. It was a natural state of being, one she'd grown accustomed to and one which would allow him to freely approach her when the time was finally right. That could be any night, such as tonight, so Gina had dressed carefully as she always did on Thursdays, and poured herbal after-bath-splash over her shoulders and neck. Her silky and thin fawn-colored hair was pulled softly back and held in place with bar-rette of silk flowers. She'd pinched her cheeks to a pink blush and used no lipstick or mascara or eyeshadow. Gary, she knew, would like a natural girl. One who had no need to paint her face or use cosmetics to conceal the per-son she was inside. That was just one of the many special things about Gary. He was sensitive, aware. Not at all like the other men Gina had known.

True, Gina had not personally met Gary or spoken to him. But she knew him, nonetheless. After six months of Thursdays, sitting in the cafe and listening to him play, hearing his fluid voice sing about gentle love, she knew him well. Her favorite song was the one in which he de-scribed how their life would be together, "with two cats in the yard, life used to be so hard, now everything is easy 'cause of you ..."

Gina savored each note and word that issued from his lips. Here was a man who treasured the things that really mattered in life. The purity of each morning, the kiss of the sun on bare skin, the simple existence of animals and plants. "Our house is a very, very fine house ..."

He saw beyond the obvious and clear through the phony and hypocritical facade of most people. Gary was capable of understanding her and, by now, was probably already in love with her.

Since February, Gina had been sitting at one of the tables, inconspicuously taking notes with a gold-tipped fountain pen while he sang. The waiter who brought her refills of herbal tea thought Gina was doing homework from the book that lay open in front of her. But that was only a prop.

From the night's notes, Gina would compose poetry. Beautiful words she knew Gary would understand and appreciate. In the back of her mind, she hoped he would one day sing some of those words in a song he'd write just for her. She sent him the poems she'd written. Once every week or two she'd mail an envelope sealed with violet wax to the P.O. box on the business cards Gary left at the cashier's stand in the cafe. Of course, she never signed the poems.

Once, her heart nearly stopped when Gary sang an original piece and one phrase echoed her poetry. "The breeze blows your voice to me and leaves dance beneath the trees - like an autumn night you steal my summer soul ..." and so on. It was a sign.

Most of the other people in the audience chatted while Gary sang. Some of the sillier girls, probably from the nearby city college, giggled and talked about him. They flashed him glossy smiles painted with peach and apricot lipsticks and batted their flashing eyes framed with powders and liners and thickened lashes. From the stage, Gary acknowledged their attention with a shy grin but, being a professional, he went no further. Gina knew they were definitely not his type.

She endured the silliness of the other girls and exercised patience. Patience was her greatest virtue. She figured she had very little to thank her mother for, but the ability to wait and bide her time had been one of the few gifts she'd gotten from her childhood. That, and the house with its sprawling land and wild garden. Gary would love her house because it was very much like the one he sang about; "Such a cozy room, the windows are illuminated." She smiled picturing the parlor in her house.

Gina was surprised when she'd found out the house was hers. She'd had no idea how those things worked and really never thought about what she'd do once Mother was gone from her life. It had worked out remarkably well. She'd immediately thrown out all the nick-knacks and fringe, all the garish torchiere lights and mini blinds. She pulled up the plush champagne carpet and exposed the old hardwood floor. At a swap meet, she sold all the brass and glass tables, velvet upholstered dining chairs, molded plastic TV trays and generally anything that revealed her mother's taste for the cheap and counterfeit.

Now, the tiny one bedroom house on the three-acre lot that backed up to the shopping center where the bookstore was located, looked nothing like her mother. Gina draped lace around the windows for curtains and installed old-fashioned shades with satin rope pulls. The couch was plush green velvet with a high back and wide arms. She'd covered up the holes where the cotton filling was pushing through with a crocheted blanket. Small rugs were displayed on the floor and an old rug from Pakistan covered the path she walked from the front door to the kitchen.

All the furniture was vintage or antique. Found at rummage sales or salvaged from someone else's trash heap. But, the furnishings were lost to the eye amid the constant display of flowers that adorned each shelf, window sill, table, and surface in Gina's house. No matter what the season, Gina picked and arranged dozens of bouquets of flowers that compelled the outdoors to enter each room and dominate with color and smells.

There were vases filled with roses and carnations, ranunculus, daisies, tall and elegant Queen of the Nile blooms, and a circular bed where a tall cactus stood like a monolith surrounded by succulents that bloomed with color in the early summer. What never appeared indoors was the Bird of Paradise flowers. Though Gina had a small plot of the colorful and dramatic single flowers, she never cut them. The sharply pointed petals and almost artificial beauty of the blooms reminded Gina of her mother.

The great display of color was easy to harvest, for most of the acreage (the last, large plot in the urban zone) bloomed with a riot of flowers. The perimeter of tall oleander bushes obscured the garden beds that appeared planted without regard for order or landscape design. Like a patchwork quilt, spring daffodils sprung up next to a bed of baby's breath. Large rows of perennials produced nearly constant blooms in a rotation according to the season. Although the entire yard was planted in a seemingly helter-skelter fashion, it was, nonetheless, brilliant, beautiful and purposeful.

Gina walked along the winding dirt paths among the beds of flowers and gathered fresh bouquets. She was sometimes followed by one of many cats that adopted her garden as a sanctuary from the asphalt and traffic that bordered the property. She had taken great care to protect the cats, not only from the surrounding urban dangers but from accidents that might happen in her own yard. She learned her lesson when the sleek black female she'd named Virtue had been poisoned by eating some of the special herbs in her garden. Now, the fertile bed was covered with clear plastic, draped on a wire frame. Not only were the cats safe, the makeshift greenhouse produced herbs all year long. She'd buried Virtue near her house and planted a scarlet fuchsia over the grave. It produced a profusion of flowers in spring, and each Easter, Gina cut a single bough, brought it inside and put it in a crystal vase on the kitchen table.

In summer and early fall, butterflies danced over her head and hummingbirds dined on the nectar of the blossoms that turned the entire yard into a fragrant rainbow.

At first, people were curious about the little house and large garden. Some tried to talk with Gina and get her to show them around. That was when Gina had a six-foot high, chain link fence installed. At first, it had been a necessary eyesore, but by now all the ugly metal was overtaken by climbing ivy, wisteria, and other vines. Her privacy was nearly complete, except for the persistent agents who continued to leave business cards wedged into her wooden front gate. Gina had no intention of selling her property. Not at any price though some had been bold enough to scrawl seven-figure offers on the backs of their cards. Gina could never leave, of course. Her history and her future were forever intertwined with all that lived and died and been renewed in her garden.

The house itself was not worth much. It was old and showing the signs of time and neglect. Gina was a far better gardener than carpenter and she'd given up trying to repair eaves infected with dry-rot or the roof that leaked with each winter's rain. She knew something would have to be done in the near future, but she'd been loath to let strangers past the gate from their world into hers. At any rate, she figured that Gary would know what to do once he came there to live with her.

Until then, she concentrated on improvements that camouflaged the deteriorating structure. Most of this she accomplished with the cacophony of flowers and other decorations that covered up imperfections.

On the walls were old photos, black and white, hand tinted pictures of people from the turn of the century in the days before televisions and computers had invaded homes. Antique frames held similar family portraits on the mantle over the fireplace. They were not photos of Gina's family. She had no idea who the people were and didn't really care. On one wall, she'd hung an old guitar with the graceful hummingbird artfully embossed on the finger guard. It was waiting for Gary's touch. Of course, she'd make room for more of his things which, she was sure, would fit the decor she'd carefully nurtured.

In a silver bowl tucked behind two photos framed in old silver, were several business cards from the persistent realtors. Gina kept them because she realized (though she didn't care) that they represented monetary value. That reminder was important because money was something her mother was forever looking for in the men who came to the house. It made Gina laugh to realize the money had been there all along, under their feet.

Gary began his set with a ballad. Gina felt a physical warming that started in the small of her back and traveled through her belly and into her chest. It was pleasant and she smiled at him. Each Thursday he'd acknowledge her at least once - look right at her and return the warm smile. After so many weeks, he couldn't help but notice her constancy.

Two women walked in and noisily took the table next to Gina's. Once their paper bags were settled, the women proceeded to discuss the menu and waved down the server with a rude shout that drowned out Gary's music. Gina glared at them. One was blond, the other a brunette. Both were wearing heavy makeup and designer clothes. The large shopping bags sported the Nordstrom's label. They laughed too loudly and put their heads together to tell some hushed secret. Gina didn't like them, particularly the blond with her hair piled on top of her head, dark roots showing around the hairline. The woman looked like someone Gina knew, but couldn't immediately place. The blue eyeshadow, the crimson lips, the plum blusher carried high on the cheekbones. All that makeup was meant to cover something the woman was hiding. No purity, no innocence.

Gina's mother had tried to convince her to wear makeup. She used to give Gina sample bottles she'd picked up in department stores and once, after drinking a few glasses of clear liquid, had made Gina sit down in front of a vanity mirror for a makeup session. Her mom's latest boyfriend sat on the bed and watched, clutching a half-empty bottle and smoking an unfiltered cigarette. Gina couldn't remember how old she'd been, but she knew the other girls at her school had not begun to paint their faces and the experience felt vaguely forbidden. Mother had been in a fine mood, however, and Gina didn't protest as creams and liquids and pencils touched her soft skin and tickled. Gina's eyes, her mother had said, were her best feature. Eye make up would take attention away from other, less attractive features such as her too large nose and thin lips.

It had seemed like hours that she'd sat on the stool in front of the oval mirror. Finally, a stranger's image stared back at her. A little girl with a woman's face, lips drenched in bright red and eyes set in hazy shadows. Her mother had piled Gina's hair on top of her head, exposing an ivory neck that didn't blend with the painted portrait in the mirror.

"Don't she look great?" her mother said to the boy-friend. "That's my lil' girl there. Gonna be a man-killer af-ter she gets a figure, just like her mom, huh, sweetie." She leaned back to admire her work and sipped her drink from the kitchen glass. A slow smiled crawled across her face and she turned to the man on the bed. "Now don't you go gettin' any ideas, hear? Under all that paint, she's still lil' plain Jane." She laughed and drank some more.

The man thought it was funny too, and as Gina tried to ease out of the room, he caught her by the arm and pulled her to him. The boyfriend smelled bad and his breath was rank with smoke. He set the bottle on the end table and picked up the guitar that had been lying on the bed beside him. He liked to strum the guitar and follow Gina's mother around the house singing songs about love. Sometimes it was fun, but the singing usually turned ugly as he got louder and the words became silly words that Gina didn't fully understand.

The boyfriend always wore blue denim shirts, jeans and pointed cowboy boots with silver decorating the toes. There was a shock of greasy blond hair that fell over his forehead, and Gina's mom was forever brushing it out of his eyes.

"Honey, you do look good. Don't let your mom fool you," he said through a haze of cigarette smoke. "See, honey, she's jus' afraid of a lil' younger woman." He opened his mouth wider and spit out a laugh that became a cough. Gina noticed the man's teeth were dark and crooked and that his breath smelled dirty. He twisted her small body and slid an arm around her waist, so Gina couldn't get away. He pulled her in close while he took another long drink from the tall, clear bottle on the bed stand.

"Why mama, she's just an armful," he said to Gina's mother. "Come on over here, sugar. I got two good arms."

Gina's mom laughed from her throat and sauntered over to the bed. The boyfriend shifted Gina over to his side in order to wrap his free arm around her mother.

28

"Now you, you sugar, are more than a handful," he said and buried his face in the folds of the robe Gina's mom was wearing.

The nuzzling and guttural noises continued. Her mom laughed and squealed at first, petting his rough beard with her hand. Gina knew what the beard felt like because he sometimes gave her a little kiss on the cheek and followed up by rubbing his chin against her soft skin. It was like a nasty cactus plant. Painful and ugly. She could not understand why her mom would want to touch such a face.

Gina struggled to get away. "Where you think you're goin' lil' missy with the ruby red lips?" he taunted, holding her more tightly. "You ain't goin' anywhere. You already got a date."

The boyfriend pulled both Gina and her mom down on the bed with him. The couple laughed in unison, although Gina could find nothing funny at all. He whispered some words she couldn't hear and her mom reached down and unbuckled the man's belt. "Gonna give you a lesson now that you look so grown up," she said with a thick tongue. "You jus' watch."

Gina closed her eyes. Horrid sounds began to fill the bedroom, but the boyfriend didn't let her go. In fact, he grabbed her tighter in places she hated being touched. Gina tensed every bone in her body and covered her ears with her hands. The moaning finally stopped and when Gina looked, her mother had fallen asleep, her long hair spread across the man's lap. The boyfriend turned his head and showed his blackened teeth. "Gonna take a quick five," he said, breathing the breath of a serpent into Gina's face. "Then we'll see if you learned anything."

All those memories came back to Gina as she looked at the women, particularly the one with the upswept hair. Suddenly, she could not keep the image of her mother from superimposing itself on the stranger's face. Gina stared into her cup of tea and felt the steam rise, cleansing her. Purging. They were gone now. All of them, Gina said to herself. All the boyfriends with their rough hands and rougher ways. Her mother, with her weakness and colored fingernails. Her paint and satin robes. Her laugh that bubbled like a bottle of shaken beer.

"Life used to be so hard," she silently sang to herself and returned her attention to Gary. Of course, life was not like the song. Everything was not "easy." But it was no longer ugly. She had her garden and its special places that produced great beauty. From the barren earth, she'd nurtured splendor and camouflaged a dark past. She could bring the beauty inside to exorcise the demons that had once lived there.

Gina had enough money to easily get by and had no desire for material things. Her main expense was replacing plants and buying new varieties for her garden that flourished throughout the year. There were also gardening supplies, cat food, minor tools and other such modest acquisitions. Everything was going to work out fine, she assured herself. Patience was her friend. She'd even named her favorite, white, long-haired cat, Patience.

"It wonderful stuff. You put it on over your makeup and the lines under your eyes just go away," the woman with upswept hair was saying to her friend. Though their heads were close together like conspirators, her voice was shrill and easily carried to Gina's table. "It's thirty bucks a jar, but hell, that's cheaper than plastic surgery, although I think that's already on my calendar." The other woman laughed and said, "Here's to middle age and the miracles of modern medicine." The pair touched their wine glasses together in a toast.

Gina wasn't interested in their conversation and resented how they so easily ignored the music. Gary was playing a fiery instrumental now, one born of the tormented spirit of pure flamenco. He knocked his thumb on the front of the guitar, rapping out an urgent rhythm behind the allegro notes he picked with his fingers. Mercifully, the women stopped their chattering.

Gina was inspired to write some words about a "pounding heart" and the " anguished cry" of a woman about to be swallowed by the sea. She felt the partnership with Gary even more acutely in these moments when his music moved her to write.

He kept his eyes focused on his right hand that picked the strings with blinding speed and his head cocked to one side, pulling the neck of the guitar close to his ear. Gary was pure concentration and intensity. His music pierced the banal reality of cafe culture and swept it away to the Iberian Peninsula with a timeless, ageless melodic heartbeat. Gina was drawn away from her notebook and compelled to watch as tiny beads of sweat appeared on Gary's brow. She felt a warming through her body that spread like slow honey. It was a dangerous feeling, she knew, but she let it flow until it was no longer bearable and then ended it by poking the end of the fountain pen into the palm of her hand, drawing a spot of blood.

Back in control, she glanced over at the women - prisoners too, of Gary's passion. The upswept blond cupped her hand over the other woman's arm as if to keep herself from being carried aloft by the music. To the ear it sounded like two, perhaps three, guitarists were playing the counter melodies and rhythms.

The piece crescendoed to an end, the complex melody punctuated with hard, rapid raps against the guitar. For a long moment there was silence, as if the audience could still hear the notes ringing, weaving a story of torment and romance. Then, there was an eruption of applause which Gary acknowledged by slowly raising his head and gazing at the small crowd with a shy smile. It is how he must look when he wakes up in the morning, Gina thought.

This was the end of his first set and Gary would say a few modest words, inviting people to drop a dollar or two in the jar that stood on the edge of the raised platform where he performed. This was obviously hard for him and Gina ached for Gary every time he had to make the pitch for money. When he was with her of course, he wouldn't have to do that anymore.

It was also a time when he surveyed his audience and

32

Gina had caught his eye more than once. It was always exciting to think about.

The women came back to life and the blond laughed loudly when her friend said something tasteless about "taking a cold shower." "Honey, I prefer hot showers," she answered, "if you know what I mean."

Gary glanced across the floor and paused when he spotted Gina in her usual spot. She sent him a silent message in that split second, as she always did. But his eyes were drawn away too quickly by the peel of the blonde woman's laughter and Gina felt cheated, angry at them.

As he leaned down and tucked his guitar into its case, the women chattered to each other in hushed voices. Gina heard only a few words here and there. Words like "hunk," and "I'd like to get my hands on..." They were clearly the kind of women that Gina would never be. Could never be.

Gary rose from the wooden stool and looked in Gina's direction. Her heart nearly stopped as he stepped down from the stage and walked her way. She felt the pounding in her chest, like the intense raps from the heels of a flamenco dancer. All thoughts and words fled from her mind and a dizziness filled her head as Gary neared her table. The blue and gold pen slipped from her fingers, and her palms grew wet with perspiration. Her eyes could not leave his face and finally, she was looking directly up at him, her mouth slightly open as if to say something, although no words were available to her.

He paused and smiled. "Hi, how ya doin'? Thanks for

coming again. I appreciate it," he said to her before taking two more steps and sitting down at the women's' table.

For a time, Gina neither heard nor saw anything. She was frozen in body and spirit, unable to move or think or react. Slowly, the cafe crept back into her consciousness and the conversation grated against her senses. "Baby, I've been tellin' my friend Cheryl here all about you," the up-sweep was saying. Gary was grinning.

"I hope you didn't tell her any of my trade secrets, did you?" he answered.

"Those are just between you and me and the camera," the blond giggled.

Gina continued to feel dizzy. She tried to grab control of pieces of herself that were spinning out of her body, into dark space. She wanted to cast out the conversation but helplessly took in the worst of it.

"Cheryl wants to play, honey." The upsweep now had nuzzled in closer to Gary and was making little tracks up the front of his shirt with her viscous red nails.

"Did you tell Cheryl that there's a players' fee?" Gary intoned, looking now at Cheryl.

"I hear you're a good investment," she responded. "I'll take it out of my entertainment budget."

As suddenly as it had settled upon her, the dizziness stopped and Gina was visited by profound clarity. She heard all the words of the trio dealing at the next table, and all the conversations of everyone in the cafe. She felt all the pain, silliness, discomfort, sorrow, giddiness of the collective patrons and saw all of them for who they were. A calm settled and Gina followed the negotiations for Gary's attention. She wasn't surprised or horrified when they began to use forbidden words that Gina hadn't heard since Mama's last boyfriend whispered them to her. It was all settled, and she knew that Gary needed rescuing. He needed to be where he belonged. With Gina.

"Well. ladies. Got to get back to work," Gary was saying. "Don't forget to drop a little something in the jar when you leave."

"How about the address to my condo and a key?" Cheryl teased.

"Hey, watch it. Who discovered this stud anyway?" The blond warned. "This is a three-way partnership. Right baby?"

"For the right kind of money, I can partner anyway you want," Gary joked. "Gotta run." He stood at the table and discretely brushed himself against the blonde's arm. "Man of steel," she winked to Cheryl.

Gina knew she had to save Gary fast. It wouldn't keep until next week and, for once, he was so close by. If she were to wait until after the final set, she'd have to approach him. Maybe be one among many who wanted to talk with the guitarist. People might notice her and she couldn't allow that.

"Excuse me?" she said as Gary walked past her table. He turned and looked down at her.

"Ya?"

"Um, I wanted to tell you that, well, I really like your playing," she stammered.

"Ya, I notice you're here a lot," he answered. "Listen, I'd like to talk, but I gotta get back."

"I just want to tell you that I have something you might want," she said, hoping he didn't think for a moment that she was at all like those women next to her. "It's a guitar. A rare guitar. A 1962 Gibson Hummingbird."

"Where'd you get that?" he asked, obviously impressed. "That's worth a few grand."

"I know. About six, to be exact," she said, growing in confidence. "It was left to me by an uncle and I don't play. I don't really need it and I've been thinking that I'd like you to have it."

"Have it, like in for free?" He said with a smile crawling across his face.

"That's what I mean," she said, satisfied. "You're so talented and I'd know the instrument is going to a really worthy person. My uncle would have liked that."

"Man, what can I say?"

"You don't have to say anything," she added. "Just come over to my house and get it."

"Great! Anytime! You name it," he said and leaned a hand on her table.

Gina picked up her pen and then put it back on the

table. "Actually, I don't have to write it down. It's just on the other side of this shopping center. The only house left in the whole area. There's lots of tall oleander and vines around it. Real easy to find. How about this Sunday afternoon at, say two o'clock?"

"Sound's perfect. Hey, thanks a lot ... I didn't even get your name."

"It's Gina – for Angelina," she smiled. " And, you're welcome."

He turned and strutted back to the platform where he picked up his guitar and began another set. He started with an upbeat piece that, Gina laughed, probably reflected his recent set of personal triumphs.

She scribbled on her writing pad, loops and more loops that became flowers. She thought about how Gary had so quickly believed she would simply give him such a valuable guitar. But arrogant people were like that. Like showy hybrids with no scent that bloomed and died within the span of only a few days.

She gathered up her writing materials, set the cup on its saucer and dropped the used tea bag inside. There was no longer a need to stay in the cafe. The music had lost its allure. And, there were things to be done in preparation for Gary's visit. She'd polish the guitar, straighten the house, put fresh bouquets throughout and carefully set the low coffee table where they'd have tea together. Then, perhaps, she'd let Gary touch the guitar. Gina had everything she'd need. The special herb was growing in the garden. This she'd add to the flavorful tea blend that was her very own recipe. The one her mother and that last boyfriend had liked so much. "Make us a pot of that tea of yours, Gina baby," her mom would say. "Just leave it on the floor outside my bedroom door like a good girl."

Gina wrapped a shawl around her shoulders and stepped out into the waning evening light that reflected softly on the blacktop of the parking lot. Block upon block of asphalt, she thought and contrasted that with her oasis of flowers. Her sanctuary where Mama and the boyfriend would never harm her again, where they were lovely in the springtime.

She closed her eyes and left the warm air drift over her face. What kind of flower was Gary, she pondered. Beautiful on the outside, passionate, precious, but fragile. A flower that bloomed quickly and then, just as quickly, faded and died. "A rose," she said aloud. "A Blue Angel Face Rose." Unlike many blue varieties, it was fragrant and Gina thought she'd put a small bouquet on the table next to her brass bed. There, she could wake up to the sweet, seasonal scent of Gary. She began to plan where he would grow in her garden.

Beyond the Garden Path

Gina rose slowly from her knees and looked over the bed of spring annuals she'd just planted. As always, the rewards of a few hours in the garden were more than satisfying - they were inspiring, fortifying. They were, in fact, a reason to live.

Over the seventy-some years of her life, Gina had seen more than her share of darkness. Always at the hands of other people who somehow meant her harm. A plant had never disappointed or frightened her. Even when they died away she was not saddened because it was a natural order that fed the soil and gave birth to more beauty.

Gina had lived on three acres in the middle of an urban zone on the flat, hard-pan earth in a Central California city for her entire life, except for a few months as a young child when her mother had taken up with a truck driver. Then, Gina vaguely recalled sleeping on a hard seat high up in the cab of a truck and looking silently out a window as endless miles of highway rolled by taking her to nowhere and back again. Funny, Gina mused as she wiped her wrinkled hands on her gardening apron, that she hadn't remembered much of that early-on time until now when she was an old woman. Now she recalled lots of things from childhood that she would just as soon forget.

Like how her flaxen hair, the color of the hillsides of the great valley from May to November fell in natural ringlets around her face. Her mother had been very proud of Gina's hair, commenting on it to the boyfriends who moved in and out of their lives like hungry strays.

Gina still liked her eyes, which were a radiant Lapis blue on a field of bright white. As her once doll-like face had changed with age, the color of her eyes remained the same.

She'd retained her youthful complexion into her late fifties. This Gina credited to never having polluted her face with make-up. For decades her skin breathed pure air, her pores free of chemicals. But eventually gravity won and her youthful skin surrendered to time.

Gina looked down. A big calico cat wove between her feet and sashayed over to Blossom the mutt who laid sleeping in the shade of an oleander bush. Gina once had dozens of cats. Every stray that could make it across busy

42

Blackstone Avenue seemed to find her place, creating a haven for wandering felines. Gina once thought of it as her "cathouse" but knew the nasty implication was unworthy of her.

She'd gone to extreme measures to accommodate those cats. Built special fences to keep them inside her compound, little greenhouses to keep them outside of her herb bed which had once claimed the life of Virtue, her favorite black cat.

Now, all she had left was Pansy the calico and that pesky dog - more of a necessity than a pet - thanks to that busybody woman from the Mexican restaurant in the shopping center that backed up to her property. What did they expect, Gina thought, remembering the event nearly a decade ago. Throw perfectly good food out the back door. Pile meat and fish scraps in open garbage cans. What self-respecting cat isn't going to take advantage of a meal like that?

The woman had hollered over the fence, picked up a scraggly orange tabby and flung it like litter through the bushes back onto Gina's property. Wanting to avoid attention, Gina had done everything humanly possible to keep the cats on her side of the fence. She fed them canned food, strung chicken wire on loose parts of the fence, sprayed "Cat-Away" along the border but, of course, the smell of crab and chicken, carne asada and ceviche wafting from the food piles was more powerful than her preventative measures. The woman continued to launch cats over the fence, screaming some words in Spanish that

Gina couldn't understand.

Then, one day, the cat crisis reached a climax. Gina was working on her roses, lovingly removing the aphids from the young buds with a soapy solution, when the woman screeched like a banshee. She started yelling in Spanish and then switched to English. "Hijola, los gatos! Ayudame. Cinco gatos! I know you hear me ober there," she shouted across the fence. "You are there and you jus leesen to me. I hab five gatos at my door. Cinco! I yam going to march right over to your house right now an give you a beeg piece of my mind!"

Gina dropped her spray bottle and sponge. She ran straight to the front of her property and stood to the side of the six-foot-high gate that protected her fortress from outsiders. She had no intention of letting the woman in and wondered how to make the whole situation go away. Within ten minutes there was a banging on the gate and Gina froze. "Ees me, from the restaurant! I know you hear me. Eef you don' open up and talk to me bout thees, I will call police. You shoose."

Gina could picture the woman standing there in the brutal afternoon sun with her arms folded across her chest and jaw set with determination.

The last thing, besides nosey neighbors, that Gina wanted was the police on her property. She couldn't let that happen. Gina opened the gate slightly. The woman, portly and short with a brightly colored scarf tied around her head, and a face flush with heat and anger, stood anchored to the spot.

44

"Well. What you gonna do? You gonna get rid of those cats? They make beeg mess at my place where I work. The boss, he gets mad at me. Well!?"

Gina found her voice and politely told the woman she would take the cats to the shelter the coming week. There were so many, she explained, it would take a few trips.

Gina, of course, had no intention of taking the cats anywhere. She didn't even own a car much less have the desire to hand her cats over to strangers who would probably treat them cruelly.

"Let me tell you. You don' hab them gone by thees weekend, we gonna call the police. I am bery serious. I don' wan to lose my job for no gatos."

The woman glanced past Gina into the yard. "Nothin' personal," she added as a sort of apology. "You got some pretty flowers there."

The plan came to Gina like ants to honey. "I understand," Gina said. "I really am sorry for trouble the cats might have caused you. Why don't you just step inside and let me give you a few flowers to take back? As a peace offering?"

"Well, that would be nice," the woman said stepping through the gate and onto the stone path that meandered past the tiny house and through the acres of flowers. "Ees not I don like cats. One, two cats, hokay. Unnerstan?"

"I understand perfectly," Gina answered and moved slowly down the path. "How about some yellow daisies and some of that baby's breath around a few roses?"

"Thas nice, but please don' be thinkin' I change my mind about the cats. The jeffe, he be very mad with me when he see the mess they make in the back. He fire me eef it happen again." The woman's anger seemed to have softened but Gina had no choice. The stranger was in her garden. She'd threatened to call the police. Gina picked up the short handled shovel she used for planting shrubs and leaned on it like a cane.

"You won't have to worry about the cats anymore, I promise," she said to the woman. "Would you mind handing me those gardening shears by your feet?"

"Sure," the woman answered bending down for the blue handled snippers. "Ees not personal theeng weeth me, I ....."

Her sentence, filled with the timber of apology ended with a ringing thud as Gina brought the flat blade of the shovel down on the woman's head. She fell unconscious into the bed of Shasta daisies, bending the bright flowering branches of one plant to the ground. Gina quickly rolled the body off the plant and onto bare dirt, rescuing the damaged branches. She then pulled the scarf from the woman's head before dealing two more blows. If she wasn't already dead, she would be helpless long enough for Gina to dig an appropriate grave. Then, she'd make sure to finish the job with the pointed end of the shovel.

It was early evening when Gina was completely done. With a bed of mature Mexican Heather transplanted from other parts of her garden, it would soon be impossible to tell that the area had been recently disturbed.

46

Later that night, Gina left her compound carrying an old canvas bag over her shoulder and walked around the block to the shopping center where cars still filled the parking lot. Near the corral where customers left their shopping carts, not too far from the restaurant, she dropped the bag to the ground, removed the colored scarf and stuffed it inside one of the carts. No one had bothered to watch because Gina was very practiced at being inconspicuous - a drab older woman as nondescript as any. Having studied people from a distance, she knew that beggars and street people, down-and-outers collecting cans and bottles, made shoppers uncomfortable. In fact, they purposefully avoided making eye contact with those who lived on the frayed margins of civility.

Gina pretended to pick up what she had dropped, cast a glance around her and was quite satisfied she'd drawn no one's attention. For a moment, she entertained the idea of actually going into the supermarket to buy the cans of cat food she needed but decided that would be foolish. She'd return the following day wearing more mainstream attire to do the shopping. It was a trip she was dreading and she cursed the woman under the heather for making it necessary.

But then, Gina understood that life was hard. She had learned very early that fairy tales existed only on the pages of books with fanciful illustrations. Yes, there was the one time, when she'd let herself believe in a knight on a white horse - in her case, it had been a singer with a guitar - but that ending had turned out nothing like the storybooks she once read before she understood. Sometimes,

47

she laughed at how well it had actually ended. Unlike so many other women, she at least had something to show for her dedication and devotion. She had the splendid blue rose which produced prodigiously three, sometimes four, times a year. And, she'd chosen the variety carefully. Unlike most blue roses (which were actually a lavender color) this one emitted a lovely scent which she enjoyed in a vase placed strategically next to her bed.

From Gary, she had learned a lesson that guided the rest of her life. Trust no one, question all feelings, protect yourself, be prepared for disappointment. All these realizations were not new. She had been training to accept them throughout her childhood and adolescence. Her mother and her mother's boyfriends had been her instructors for an advanced degree. Only, for a few months, she'd forgotten and let herself fall in love with Gary.

Gary with the hypnotic voice and fingers that made music as beautiful as nature herself. The man who glanced right at her during his performances and knew, even though she'd only approached him through unsigned poetry written just for him, knew that Gina was his destiny. That was, of course, until those women with crimson lips and fingernails lured him in. Played on his weakness - the weakness of all males - and Gina had to stop him from going down that path. Better for him to be growing more beautiful, year after year in her garden, than to become like other men. Mama's men. She could still see Gary, sitting on the brocade chair in her dark living room, sipping the special herbal tea and holding the valuable guitar she'd promised to give him. He'd fallen asleep peacefully,

48

with little visible pain. Monkshood was like that. It was much more humane than the Palma Christi she'd used on Mama and the cactus-faced boyfriend. She'd learned from that.

And, in her garden, they all had become far more enjoyable than they'd once been, although she had missed Gary's music for a very long time. The Bird of Paradise which marked her mother's resting place was complex, exotic, beautiful, yet dangerous with its pointed petals and leaves. The boyfriend grew into a prickly pear cactus which bloomed a single, short-lived flower just once a year and Gary, well, Gary was her prize blue rose.

There were others who had come to her garden since then. Regrettable necessities to protect the sanctuary she'd built over the many years. Unlike the first three to be planted, there had been nothing personal - or creative, really - about their transformations. They had, however, been more complicated since one particularly aggressive intruder had left a car parked not far from her property.

A profuse bed of Impatiens marked the resting place of that persistent real estate agent who just wouldn't leave Gina alone, wouldn't take `no' for an answer. When the valuable piece of urban land had passed from her mother's estate into her hands, Gina had been inundated with offers from realtors. Strangely, as she refused to sell the last large piece of property in the predominantly retail district, the offers had become more generous. Enough for Gina to be a wealthy woman. But, money meant nothing to her and the sanctuary meant everything - her past, her future, her present, her freedom.

This particular real estate agent just wouldn't quit. Gina had at first ignored the constant business cards left on her gate and in her mailbox. Then the woman started banging on the gate with her fist and, even though Gina was rude to her, returned every few days. Finally, there was the act that forced Gina to cut short the woman's career in real estate. Gina had been digging a pond for water plants and Koi fish when the woman simply walked into the yard. The gate had been open so that Gina could haul yard waste to the curb and the agent couldn't resist the opportunity.

To compensate for her rude intrusion, the agent bubbled with good cheer as Gina seethed with anger. It hadn't been hard for Gina to get the woman, who was more than eager to please, to stoop down over the newly dug pond to help lay a sheet of black plastic inside the hole. One swipe with the wide end of the pickax was all it took.

Gina forever resented the loss of her Koi pond and hadn't been able to muster up the enthusiasm to do it all over again. The perfect place was taken. And, the woman had left her Mercedes parked in front of Gina's place. Since she didn't drive, Gina had arranged for someone else to take it away.

She waited until after dark and wearing her gardening gloves, cracked open the window and simply left the keys in the ignition. Car theft in the valley was a major industry. By morning, the Mercedes was gone and stripped to a shell, abandoned in an irrigation ditch behind a raisin processing plant.

The Saint, as Gina had come to think of her, had been far easier. Why some people chose to make her a personal project, she never understood, but the Saint was dedicated to Gina's salvation. One Sunday after the next for a period of many weeks, the Saint came calling with her Bible tucked between her right arm and pillowy breast. She wore silly hats and carried an upholstered bag brimming with religious literature over one shoulder. A simulated leather handbag was slung on her wrist. Gina pictured her as some sort of mahogany, human hall-tree.

The Saint would wave her Bible over her head like a red flag for Gina to see. She'd spout scripture, shouting sections from Luke that spoke of brotherly love. That last day, she'd stationed herself outside the gate for a long session. "You'll come speak the word of the Lord with me today, my friend," she'd shouted. "Ah am prepared to send my songs of praise to you throughout this glorious day that GOD HAS GIVEN!"

It happened on a day that Gina needed all her concentration to transplant several delicate Queen of the Niles. Transplanting was like surgery and the traumatized plants needed critical handling and a positive atmosphere. This did not, according to Gina, include the voice of a bad soprano warbling "Bringing in the Sheep" - the Saint's first selection for the day. Of course, all that bellowing also threatened to attract unwanted attention. Gina decided to dig the bed about three feet deeper than she had origi-

51

nally planned.

The Saint had launched into "The Old Rugged Cross" when Gina unlocked the gate and invited her in. For many months after, when Gina looked at the bright orange blossoms of the lilies, she recalled the expression on the Saint's face when the gate opened. "Praise the Lord," she had said. "The Lord has heard my prayers and opened the gates. Bless you, sister!"

After Gina explained she would have to keep working, the Saint dropped her load of books and brochures and cassette tapes on the ground, and pitched in to dig with a garden trowel, all the while talking, preaching. It had been too easy, almost regrettable. The Saint now nurtured a lovely bed of pink carnations.

Not regrettable was the scallywag who apparently thought Gina's house held treasures he might like to have for himself. The intruder had climbed the chain link fence at night, pushed his way through the thick barrier of oleander and broken a window in the living room. It was his misfortune to shatter the glass right over the little wooden table where the long-haired orange cat slept. Poppy, startled and incensed, bolted from the table and leaped onto Gina's chest as she slept in her bed. Gina knew immediately that something was wrong but never once considered calling the police. She quietly slipped out of bed and peered into the shadowy living room where she saw the man carefully easing himself through the broken shards of glass that framed the window.

"Fool," Gina thought and slipped out of her bedroom

in a low crouch, to the kitchen and into the mudroom. There, she grabbed the short handled pitchfork she used for mulching, and a can of Black Flag Insect Spray that she only used in emergencies. Gina tried to be as organic as possible in her handling of garden pests.

Peeking into the living room, she watched as the skinny form of the burglar moved toward the sideboard in the dining area. He quietly pulled open the beveled glass doors and began rummaging through the contents. His invasion of her sanctuary filled Gina with fury. Some miserable, emaciated, unethical scrap of humanity was touching her things. She was poised to act when he picked up a delicate centerpiece Gina had ordered from a catalog - a cascade of colorful roses formed in fine china. She quietly watched as he stuffed the piece into a bag slung over his shoulder. Once confident she could save the piece from destruction, Gina noiselessly crept up behind the burglar and, when close enough to feel the nervous heat from his body said, "Excuse me!"

He spun around and Gina quickly sprayed a blast of Black Flag in his face, aiming directly at his eyes. As she anticipated, he raised his hands in defense and, as he did, Gina deftly relieved him of the bag holding her cherished china roses. As he began to cough and gag and double over, Gina put an end to his misery with the pitchfork. "Not even suitable for compost," she muttered, knowing there was no better place in her garden for the sorry intruder than deep beneath a compost bin.

Until the cat-hating hysterical woman from the restaurant appeared, Gina had experienced no more trouble. Her garden grew in variety and beauty, bringing her profound pleasure and something she thought of as peace. However, the cat-hater had upset the calm. The restaurant had continued to operate even though the owner was missing. The owner, not some underling as she'd portrayed herself to Gina. Other family members had taken over, hoping that someday the woman would be found. They carried on the tradition of throwing food scraps in the uncovered back bins and the cats continued to jump the fence.

The police had found the scarf in the shopping center parking lot and suspected kidnapping. For a while, the case got lots of attention - something Gina didn't need. The foraging cats at the restaurant could bring it.

She had euthanized fifteen cats as humanely as possible. She'd spared Pansy, the calico, who appeared to be too stupid to jump the fence. The Jimson Weed had come from her garden and she'd added it to their wet food. They just went quietly to sleep, no contortions or pain. The hard part had been gathering up the bodies littered over the three acres. She'd lined her Tuffy Wheelbarrow with a satin comforter and solemnly collected the cats.

Gina reverently lowered them into a common grave along the perimeter of the fence adjacent to the restaurant that had killed them. She planted broadleaf ivy that proliferated and grew over the fence, onto the ground behind the restaurant where it attracted snails and spiders. Gina felt satisfaction when she heard the workers cursing the slimy snails and swatting at the spiders which included more than a few Black Widows. Nonetheless, Gina had nightmares that involved matted fur and creatures with fangs, and dirt up their noses.

The event had also inspired her to adopt a white dog with a black patch over one eye. Blossom patrolled the perimeter of the property with a bark worthy a dog twice his size, effectively keeping cats out of her yard. Gina guessed Blossom to be a mix of Boxer and Bulldog. She eventually came to accept his presence but knew she'd never feel the affection she'd had for the cats. She fed him regularly but never bothered to actually pet Blossom or scratch him behind his upright ears. She never called him by name. In fact, the only words she had for the dog were reprimands and warnings about wandering into her flower beds.

For company, Blossom had naturally gravitated toward Pansy who seemed perfectly happy to rub up against his legs or join him in an afternoon nap. Blossom had lately taken to lounging around the cool corners of the property where the compost heap was constantly cooking. He'd been busy there throughout the morning when he heard Gina's voice in the distance, along with a new voice that he hadn't heard before. But Blossom's senses were engaged in an interesting project in the compost heap and she easily resisted the urge to investigate.

Gina didn't ordinarily respond to commotion at her front gate, but this time there was an unusual urgency to the banging and rattling, and she stood inside, listening.

"Miss Mandrake, we need to talk to you on an urgent matter," the deep voice shouted. "We're police officers. Please unlock your gate."

Gina felt her body flash freeze from the inside out. She stood paralyzed as options bounced around her head like ping pong balls in a wind tunnel. What could they want? What could they know, suspect? Should she hide? Where?

"Miss Mandrake, it's vital we talk. You may be in danger. Please open up the gate or we'll have to do it ourselves."

Danger? What could they mean, danger? Rational thought fought for its place in her mind. The visit could have nothing to do with her garden.

"Miss Mandrake, if you are there, please, don't be scared. We are here to protect you. Open the gate, please."

Gina felt the tension melting from her limbs and self-control returning. The smart thing to do was to open the gate. Be polite. They'd go away.

"Just a minute, I'm looking for the key," she hollered. "It's in my apron pocket ... someplace - silly me," she feigned a laugh. "I get so wrapped up in my flowers ... here it is."

Gina put the key in the padlock that secured the gate from the inside. The heavy wooden door swung open and two uniformed city police officers faced her.

"Good afternoon, ma'am. Sorry to disturb you. I'm Officer Rick Delgado and this is Officer Joanne Peterson. Let's just step inside here so we can give you some information."

Delgado was a dark-skinned, husky young man with eyes the color of tobacco, and his partner, a fair-haired young woman wearing no makeup at all. Gina approved and took a cautious liking to the female officer.

Just a few feet inside her gate, standing on the stone path that led to her garden, Officer Peterson handed Gina a flyer on white paper.

"This is a police artist's sketch, Miss Mandrake, of the pair who have been working scams on the elderly in town. They target folks who own property and pretty much strip them of their equity."

Officer Delgado cast a quick glance around Gina's immense yard. "Looks to me like this place would attract these guys," he said. "They find their victims through county records and you've got to be sitting on some value here."

"I have no idea what it's worth to other people, officer," Gina said brightly, "but let me assure you, I'm not a likely victim. I am a very private person."

"We're just here to alert you, ma'am," Officer Peterson said with a kind smile that warmed Gina's heart. Yes, the young woman did remind Gina of herself so many decades ago. Natural, unpainted, quietly pretty.

"A lot of people have tried to worm in here, you know, but I won't tolerate it," Gina confided, her innate confidence returning.

"Our information says you live here alone," the Officer added. "You're not frightened, backed up to the shopping center and all, no neighbors?"

"Nope. Not scared. Never have been," Gina responded, shaking her head and sticking out her chin.

Officer Delgado again let his eyes drift over the profusion of blossoms - gladiolus, daises, California Poppies, countless varieties of roses. "It's pretty impressive, what you've done here," he said, thumbs hooked to the heavy leather belt around his waist. "My dad's a gardener. I know what kind of time something like this takes."

Gina heard in that statement a hint that he'd like to look around. And, unusual as it was, she felt the urge to show the polite pair her botanical treasure - her lifetime work. Especially the young woman for whom Gina felt an inexplicable trust.

"Yes, well, it's pretty much all I do," she answered. "If you like, I'll show you my rose garden. Everything is in full bloom this time of year. The rest isn't ready for visitors." A look at the roses and she'd escort them back to the gate and out of her life.

The main rose bed was a broad strip about twenty - feet wide and nearly twice as long. Surrounded by redwood chips and a stone walkway laid on dry mortar, it received full sun for most of the day and sat as the crown jewel of her efforts. Spread before them was a rainbow of carefully planned, fist-sized blossoms of pink, crimson, white, and peach with hearts of gold and cream petals tipped with blazing orange. Nestled in between like dark shadows were long stemmed, blood-red roses. Deep beauty with a nearly intoxicating sweet scent. Only the blue rose stood alone, in a special spot near her house.

"I've never seen anything like this," the woman cop said. "It's just beautiful."

"You should open this place up to the public," Officer Delgado said. "This is a showplace!"

Joanne Peterson seemed to understand. "I think Miss Mandrake values her privacy," she said. "But you do have an unusual way with living things."

"Well, yes, I am a bit of a recluse," she answered, grateful to the young woman. "I have everything I need right here." Gina picked up her shovel. " Now, if you don't mind I'd better get back to work. Need to make use of the daylight."

The officers turned toward the gate. "Somehow I'd feel better knowing you had some protection, ma'am," Officer Delgado said, turning back to face her. "An alarm system. Something to alert you to intruders."

"Oh, but I do!" Gina said brightly, guiding the pair toward the gate. "I have Blossom. He's a good-sized dog with a good loud bark." She looked over her yard. "In fact, I can't figure why he wasn't barking when you first came up. He's very protective around me."

"Hope nothing is wrong. Want me to take a look around for him?" Officer Delgado offered.

"No"! Gina responded too quickly, sensing that old feeling of alarm creep up her spine. "No, that's not necessary. He's probably just off with the cat somewhere."

"It's no trouble," he insisted and Gina realized what a mistake it had been to part with so much personal information. Her roses. That dog. She decided to get it over with.

"I'll call him. Wait, he'll come," Gina said and inhaled deeply. "Blossom! Blossom, boy. Come here!"

Back by the compost bin, Blossom heard unintelligible shouting. "Blossom ..blah, blah...come." But since he was unused to being called and didn't know his name, he remained engaged with enticing smells wafting from the large cage of decomposing garbage and garden cuttings.

Pansy, accustomed to Gina's voice, did come. She tiptoed up, arching her back and rubbed Gina's ankles.

"Well, there's the cat," Officer Peterson observed. "Pretty thing." And she bent to scratch its back.

"I'm not feeling right about leaving you, ma'am," Officer Delgado said. "We at least need to know your dog's all right."

"Really, it's fine," Gina protested. "It's just a lazy dog. He'll show up."

"I wouldn't be able to sleep tonight," he assured her. "Let's take a quick walk. See if we can scare him up."

Gina knew there was really nothing to fear. All her special plantings were mature. Still, she kept the shovel in her hand as she reluctantly led them down the garden path, periodically calling, "Blossom" and silently cursing the dog. She kept up a good pace, not giving her escorts time to drink in the stunning beauty that surrounded them.

"I just have so much to do," Gina muttered, "that I hate to waste my time on that dog."

"I understand," Officer Delgado said. "One look around and we'll be out of here."

"Well, I do appreciate your concern, specially about the scammers," Gina said, trying to soften her voice. "I don't mean to seem ungrateful. It's just that I'm really in no danger - you have to believe me on that - and I have so much to do."

They walked over the smooth, cool stones on the path, passing wild yellow daisies surrounded by a border of deep purple pansies. They moved into the shaded area where ferns and spider plants with shoots like fireworks were thriving despite the valley heat.

"Amazing," Officer Delgado would say every now and again. "I wish my dad could have seen this." Gina heard the past-tense and was grateful the old gardener was already dead. But still, the hair on her neck bristled and she began to calculate what she would have to do ensure her future privacy.

Just past a panoramic display of pink and white Azaleas, they reached a corner of the property and Officer Peterson stopped dead in her tracks. "What's that I see over there?" she said, pointing toward the compost heap. "That looks like one dirty dog to me." The young woman smiled and looked at Gina who couldn't help but think how pretty the officer was.

Blossom looked up, unsure of what was expected of him. The instinct to stay in his smelly cache held him half-buried in a hole he'd dug under the bin.

"Blossom! Bad dog, bad dog!" Gina shouted, trying to shoo the dog away. Not understanding, he didn't budge.

"Looks scared," Officer Peterson said. Gina was touched that the officer was, obviously, an animal lover.

"Probably protecting his favorite bone," Officer Delgado added. Which was, indeed, the case. When the young cops approached the dog, however, it cowered and slinked away, back to Gina, who stood in the path clutching her pointed shovel with both hands, thinking how she'd deal with the dog when the company was gone.

The officers looked into the hole that Blossom had excavated throughout the day. "There, there's his bone," Officer Delgado laughed and pointed. "Looks like Blossom's been a busy boy!"

Officer Peterson gently placed her hand on her partner's arm. She looked directly into his eyes and nodded toward the hole. They both saw the raw bones of the ribcage and simultaneously recognized the adult femur laying on top of the pile where Blossom had apparently tossed it.

Gina caught the look that had passed between them.

62

"Try as I might, I can't keep him out of the garbage ..."

There was a moment of dead silence. "So," Gina said, "just let me show you out now that we've found him. I'm sure we all have better things to do." She turned as if her body was a magnet that would pull the young people along with her. It was too much to hope, she knew, but it was also too unthinkable to accept the other possibility, now half-buried alongside the compost pile. It had been years since she'd planted the no-good burglar far under the floor of the bin.

The officers stood fast, the man with his jaw dropped slightly open and eyes moving from the dirt to Gina's face.

It was the young woman who spoke. "I'm afraid we have a little problem here, Miss Mandrake. It looks like your dog got hold of more than a beef bone. The ones I see here are human."

"What?!" Gina shrieked and stopped in her tracks. "Why that's ridiculous!"

"Maybe so ma'am, but that's what we've got," Officer Peterson responded and turned to her partner. "Better call the M.E. and let the captain know."

"Oh, my!" Gina gasped and clutched her heart.

As Delgado snapped the radio off his belt, Peterson moved to Gina's side. "Maybe you'd better sit down, ma'am. I know what a shock this must be."

"Yes, .. I think I will," Gina murmured and moved down the path to her house, her mind searching the garden for answers it had always held in the past. She paused by her bed of herbs and leaned on the handle of the pointed shovel. "I think I might have a cup of tea."

"I'll come with you," Officer Peterson said.

"Yes, I suppose," Gina muttered having chosen her only option.

In the kitchen, she filled a tarnished copper tea kettle and put it on the old Wedgewood stove. Gina said very little and shuffled about the tiny space where late afternoon sunlight made shadows dance like ghosts on the wall.

Joanne Peterson leaned against the pantry door that had been painted a pale green, her arms folded across her chest. "Can I help you with that?" she offered. Gina declined with a shake of her head.

As the water simmered, Gina scooped herbs from a sealed container, added a pinch of Palmas Christi seeds and placed the mix into a silver tea ball. She marveled to herself that she was not angry with the young woman as she might have been. After all, her sanctuary would soon be crawling with people digging up her garden. She put the tea ball directly into the kettle and shut off the gas flame. "Would you and Officer Delgado like a cup?" she asked Officer Peterson.

Officer Peterson responded that she was none too fond of tea having been hooked on coffee at the precinct and thanked Gina, anyway. As Gina poured tea into a flowered cup and sat down at the round breakfast table, she wondered at the young woman's calm. It was not every day, she reasoned, that they found a grave in someone's garden. She sipped the tea and let her thoughts drift. There was no question about her being taken away from her home, of course. It would not be possible for her live anywhere but in the sanctuary she'd planted and nurtured. She was like the plants, herself. Rooted there.

Through wandering and foggy thoughts, She heard the young officer make a comment or two, but Gina didn't have the energy to answer. The slight dizziness she felt was almost pleasant, although she knew her final moments might bring some anguish. A flash of Mama's brief contortions entered her mind. No matter.

Like a distant echo, Gina heard the screen door slam and saw Officer Delgado float into the kitchen, moving in exaggerated slow motion.

He spoke as if from a tunnel. "Mystery solved," he said. "I called it into the M.E. and he said to look closely at the bones. Seems they dig up old Gold Rush burials around here. Said when they built the shopping center, they had a heck of a time with the historians. Anyway, I checked out the remains like he said and, sure enough, they look to be real old - more than a hundred years, at least."

"And you could tell this how?" his partner asked.

"The amount of calcium that gets replaced in the bone," he said. " It's real obvious when you know what to look for. Anyway, the medical examiner said to bring those couple of bones in but not to make a fuss. Miss Mandrake here would have the preservationists all over her place and we wouldn't want that, would we Miss Mandrake?"

Gina felt the tightness around her heart as if vines of ivy wove through her chest, pulling at the arteries, constricting the vessels. A sharp stab, like from the thorn of the boyfriend cactus pierced her back and filled her body with pain. Still, she sat expressionless, hands folded against her chest as if in prayer, eyes closed. It was a long, still minute before the officers realized that Gina was dead.

· · · · ·

Read more by Darby Lee Patterson

The Song of Jackass Creek is a mystery novel set in a small logging town in the Sierra, near the entrance to Yosemite National Park. The book is rich in characters that charm readers and absent of graphic violence—a feature that reviewers find refreshing and appealing. Here are just a few reviews from the 4.9-Star-rating Amazon rating:

This is an excellent writer!

Darby Patterson is truly a talented writer. She describes this little town sweetly without boring the reader with unimportant detail, and her descriptions are vivid. She also develops her characters fully through conversation and action so the reader becomes acquainted with the main players and can form pictures of them early in the book. Her characters' thoughts, interactions, and past activities combine to portray the culture of Redbud throughout the story, and the story itself is creative and holds surprises along the way. I too hope Ms Patterson continues to share her talents with us!

Sondra Jensen

The Song of Jackass Creek Sings!

This author's debut novel was surprisingly... awesome! Marketed as a "gentle mystery," I was skeptical that I would enjoy it, that not being my genre of choice. But this. This was one of those mysteries that's gets labeled "cozy" because there's not a ton of cursing and bloodshed and it's character driven. But don't let that fool you. This story is flesh and blood. !" All folks who enjoy a good mystery story will like this' and those that prefer their mysteries without the blood & gore will really love this. Those types of stories are actually quite difficult to find, so I'm very thrilled to honestly say I loved it and can recommend it wholeheartedly! ENJOY

Dain Alee

Please let this be the first of a series!

Wonderful book; adult without being 'R' rated, complex story and well developed characters. The people of 'Redbud' ring true and, as a native Californian, the lumber, real estate and politics are spot on. I hope this is the beginning of a series because the author has created characters you want to know better.

D. Holmes

Please Say You'll write a Sequel!

I recently read "The Song of Jackass Creek" by Darby Patterson and enjoyed it tremendously! I love mysteries and this book is definitely a mystery. But it is so much more. The characters seemed so real and I really got involved in the story. I learned so much about the area in northern California where the story is set and Darby's "word pictures" made the Redbud area come alive for me. I know I will read it again and learn more each time.

Sue Gordon

Visit: www.songofjackasscreek.com
www.darbypatterson.com
Email: darby@darbypatterson.com

If you enjoyed these short stories please visit my website to read other short stories.

And, if classic mysteries appeal to you check out my mystery novel:

"The Song of Jackass Creek" on Amazon Books or visit the website at

www.songofjackasscreek.com

Made in the USA
Columbia, SC
10 April 2018